Also by Phil Earle

Elsie and the Magic Biscuit Tin

Phil Earle

Illustrated by Jamie Littler

Orion
Children's Books

First published in Great Britain in 2016
by Orion Children's Books
an imprint of Hachette Children's Group
a division of Hodder and Stoughton Ltd
Carmelite House
50 Victoria Embankment
London EC4Y 0DZ
An Hachette UK Company

1 3 5 7 9 10 8 6 4 2

Text © Phil Earle 2016
Illustrations © Jamie Littler 2016

A catalogue record for this book is available from the British Library.

ISBN 978 1 4440 1360 3

Printed and bound in China

www.orionchildrensbooks.co.uk

*I wrote this book for my genius daughter,
Elsie, who gifted me the idea in the first
place, and also for Grandma Waterfall and
Grandpa Pete, who always keep the
biscuit tin full - P.E.*

Contents

Chapter One

Elsie loved visiting her grandma, but not for the reasons you'd imagine.

It wasn't the huge foaming
waterfall beside the house that she
liked best,

or the swing that hung from the
branches of an old, mighty tree,

or even the field full of sheep who
fed tamely from her hand.

Oh no.

What Elsie loved best was
Grandma's biscuit tin.

Not because it was the biggest.
It was no taller than a brand new
pencil.

Not because it was the shiniest.
It was old and scuffed after years of
use.

No, Elsie loved Grandma's biscuit tin for three reasons.

1.	Instead of a lid, there was a little black button on the top. One gentle touch would start a lullaby playing. The sides of the tin would open like a trap door, before spinning slowly as you picked a biscuit from its shelf.

2. The only biscuits that fitted inside the tin were Elsie's favourites. Not digestives or shortbreads or jam rings. Chocolate fingers – and chocolate was Elsie's favourite thing in the whole world.

3. Most importantly, Elsie loved the biscuit tin because it was MAGIC. No one else knew, and Elsie had no proof, but she knew there was something special about it.

Chapter Two

"Grandma," said Elsie, when the two of them were alone one day. "I know the secret about your biscuit tin."

Grandma raised her eyebrows. "Do you really?"

"Yes. I know it's magic, but I'm not sure exactly how. Can you tell me what its special powers are?"

"If I tell you, do you promise not to breathe a word to another living soul?" Grandma said.

Elsie nodded so hard her head nearly fell off.

"Do you remember the story of Aladdin, the boy who wished upon the magic lamp?" said Grandma.

Elsie's eyes lit up. "You mean I can get three wishes by rubbing the biscuit tin?"

"Not quite," whispered Grandma. "The child who finds the last chocolate finger in the tin gets to make one wish, and the magic tin will grant it." Grandma's eyes widened. "Oh, look – there's only one biscuit left. Now, who might like it? Let me see…"

"Me!" yelled Elsie. "Pleeeaaassee!"

"It's yours." Grandma grinned.
"Just don't tell your brothers.
And **don't** tell anyone what you
wished for either."

Elsie looked at the last biscuit.
One biscuit, one wish. It was lucky,
then, that there was only one thing
she *really* wanted.

"I wish for everything I touch to turn into chocolate," she said, before shoving the biscuit into her mouth.

Chapter Three

The next few minutes passed slowly.
Elsie was desperate to see if her wish
had been granted, but what if it
was just a story?

She needed to test her powers, but she had to do it somewhere her two brothers wouldn't see. If they knew she had this 'chocolate touch', they'd never leave her alone.

Elsie ran to the back door. When she gripped the handle, something wonderful happened. Before her eyes, the white plastic turned to a thick, scrumptious chocolate-brown.

Grandma's story was true!
Checking that the coast was clear,
Elsie bit into the door handle.
Her mouth filled with the most
delicious taste, better even than a
hundred chocolate fingers.

Two more bites and the handle was almost gone. One more mouthful and Elsie wouldn't be able to open the door! She teased it ajar, had one more nibble for luck, and skipped into the garden.

The next ten minutes were wonderful. It was everything she could dream of and more.

All it took was one tiny touch
and, whoooooosh, it was chocolate
time.

Finally, Elsie lay in the sunshine, confusing the sheep by grazing on chocolate blades of grass.

Chapter Four

Elsie could eat no more. Her belly
was full and her face was covered
in a smudgy chocolate beard.

Worried she'd never be able to
hide her secret from her brothers,
she crept to the waterfall to wash
the chocolate away. But each
time Elsie scooped water into her
hand, it turned to gooey chocolate
milkshake.

"Uh oh," Elsie cried. She looked down and saw the water had been replaced by oozy chocolate. The river was now running so thick and fast that it gushed over the banks...

...and straight into
Grandma's back garden.

Elsie knew she was going to be
in big trouble.

She barged through the front
gate, turning it into a huge, shiny
bar of chocolatey goodness,
before falling, hands first, against
Grandma's car.

Seconds later, every centimetre of it was pure chocolate. A sweet shop could sell it for thousands of pounds, but Elsie didn't want anything to do with it. Eating chocolate was the last thing on her mind.

It was everywhere she looked.
It covered the flowerbeds and the
bird bath, it licked its way up the
tree trunks.

The sheep got excited and sprinted down the hill, desperate to fill their bellies. Elsie tried to push one or two away, but of course as soon as she touched them...

Chocolate sheep.

Elsie was starting to panic.
Why hadn't she wished for something
different? Like a fairy who'd tidy her
room or a pixie to do her homework?

Someone tapped her on the
shoulder, and Elsie span around,
brushing the person with her hand.

There, encased in chocolate, stood Grandma, a shocked expression on her face.

Disaster!

Chapter Five

"GRAAAAANDMAAAA!"
screamed Elsie.

How could she have been so
stupid? She'd just transformed the
only person who knew about the
mysterious powers of the biscuit
tin into the biggest midnight snack
ever! How was she going to stop
the sheep munching on Grandma
instead of the grass?

Quickly, Elsie laid Grandma on her side and rolled her towards the house.

She left her propped against the wall.

Elsie sprinted to the biscuit tin. She didn't dare pick it up in case it turned into chocolate. She thought about rubbing it like a lamp, but knew that if she tried to pick up a duster… Well, you know what would happen!

She tried to remember what
Grandma had told her.

You only got a wish if there was
one biscuit left. That was all she
knew, and the biscuit tin
was empty.

Suddenly an idea jolted Elsie's brain. The biscuit tin didn't have to be empty. Grandma **always** had more supplies. Elsie ran into the kitchen, opened the cupboard door with her knee, and found a packet of fingers on the shelf.

Racing back to the lounge with the pack between her teeth, she emptied it onto the table and slid a single biscuit into the tin. She used her fingers to pick it up. The biscuit was already chocolate after all.

"I wish to turn everything chocolatey back to normal," she said. And she really did mean it.

Chapter Six

When she got back outside, Grandma hadn't moved.

Elsie inspected her carefully.
Two arms, two legs, a nose, a pair
of ears. It didn't look as if any of
her had been nibbled.

Elsie squeezed her eyes shut and reached out with her index finger, prodding Grandma gently. She closed her eyes tighter, couldn't bear to open them and find her still encased in chocolate.

"What *are* you doing with your face?" came a voice in her ears. "Do you need the toilet?"

Elsie opened her eyes to find Grandma staring at her, not a speck of chocolate to be seen.

"Grandma. You're OK!" Elsie yelled, hugging Grandma tightly.

"Well, I would be. If I wasn't being strangled," Grandma said.

"But do you feel all right?" said Elsie.

Grandma thought about it. "Well, I am a bit hungry actually. I really, really fancy some chocolate. Do you?"

Elsie felt her stomach turn.
"No, thanks, Grandma," she said.
The old lady looked confused.
Never in all her years as a grandma
had Elsie ever said no to **that**
offer.

"What about a sandwich then?
Or a cream cracker. Or maybe…
maybe we could find some jelly
babies. I might even be able to fit
them in my special biscuit tin,"
Grandma said.

Elsie shivered at the thought of
the magic tin. But she did like jelly
babies.

"I'd love some, Grandma, thank you, but … would it be OK if we ate them straight out of the bag?"

"Er…yes, of course." Grandma smiled. "Whatever you want, my darling."

And off the two of them walked, hand in hand, dreaming of full mouths and even fuller tummies.

What are you going to read next?

Have more adventures with Horrid Henry,

or save the day with Anthony Ant!

Become a superhero with Monstar,

float off to sea with Algy,

or have your very own **Pirates' Picnic.**

Grow carrots with

Lottie and Dottie,

make magic with The Witch Dog,

and cast a spell with

The Three Little Magicians.

Enjoy all the Early Readers.